Dani's Dinosaur

by Clare De Marco and Sarah Horne

W

FRANKLIN WATTS

LONDON • SYDNEY

First published in 2015 by
Franklin Watts
338 Euston Road
London
NW1 3BH

Franklin Watts Australia
Level 17/207 Kent Street
Sydney
NSW 2000

FSC
www.fsc.org
MIX
Paper from
responsible sources
FSC® C104740

Text © Clare De Marco 2015
Illustration © Sarah Horne 2015

A CIP catalogue record for this book is available
from the British Library.

ISBN 978 1 4451 3942 5 (hbk)
ISBN 978 1 4451 3945 6 (pbk)
ISBN 978 1 4451 3944 9 (library ebook)
ISBN 978 1 4451 3943 2 (ebook)

Series Editor: Jackie Hamley
Series Advisor: Catherine Glavina
Series Designer: Peter Scoulding

Printed in China

Franklin Watts is a divison of
Hachette Children's Books,
an Hachette UK company.
www.hachette.co.uk

Dani found a dinosaur
in her garden.

"Mum! There's a dinosaur over here!" shouted Dani. "Yes, and there's a dragon in my roses!" laughed Mum.

Dani put her hand near the dinosaur. It crawled slowly onto Dani's hand.

She showed it to Mum.
"Wow!" smiled Mum.
"You really did find
a dinosaur!"

9

"What do you eat?"
Dani asked the dinosaur.

The dinosaur flicked
out its long tongue and
snatched a fly. "Yuck!"
said Dani.

"Let's take your dinosaur inside," said Mum.

12

Mum and Dani found a
glass tank for the dinosaur.

Mum sprayed the tank with special water and put in some leaves and twigs.

Dani watched the dinosaur blinking in the sunshine.

"Can we keep it, please Mum?" asked Dani.

The doorbell rang. It was
Mr Brown from next door.

"I've lost Charlie, my chameleon. Have you seen him?" he asked.

"So that's what
Dani's dinosaur is!"
laughed Mum.

"Come in, he's here!"

Mr Brown was pleased
to see Charlie.

"He eats flies," said Dani.
"And crickets!" added
Mr Brown.

Mr Brown showed Dani
the box full of crickets.

"Would you like to feed him?" he asked.

"No thanks," said Dani.

"Actually, Mr Brown," said Mum, "could we borrow Charlie sometimes? He can eat the bugs on my roses!"

"No problem," said
Mr Brown.

"Perfect!" laughed Dani.

help!

Puzzle 1

Put these pictures in the correct order.
Now tell the story in your own words.
Can you think of a different ending?

curious   scared

excited

drab   colourful

bright

Choose the words which best describe each character. Can you think of any more? Pretend to be one of the characters!

Answers

Puzzle 1

The correct order is:

1c, 2b, 3a, 4e, 5f, 6d

Puzzle 2

Dani   The correct words are curious, excited.
The incorrect word is scared.

Charlie   The correct words are bright, colourful.
The incorrect word is drab.

Look out for more stories:

For details of all our titles go to: www.franklinwatts.co.uk